I Got You a Present!

Written by

Mike Erskine-Kellie & Susan McLennan

Illustrated by

Cale Atkinson

Kids Can Press

Happy birthday!

Birthdays are the best!
You get a cake, a party and …

Speaking of presents …

I wanted to get you the greatest present ever.

Something amazing.

Something unexpected.

Something that you would really love.

So I knit you some socks.

Have you ever tried knitting
birthday socks? It's really hard.
It took me six months to make
these feet treats.

When that didn't work out,
I got you something totally chill …

A ten-scoop ice-cream cone.

But carrying it was a disaster. And
I needed a present that totally rocked.

So I decided to write you a birthday jam! I practiced it all day and night.

Sadly, I made a musical mess instead of a spellbinding song.

That's when I thought of the magic kit. I bought it. Wrapped it up. And hid it in a special place where you would never find it.

And wouldn't you know it? Just like magic, it disappeared.

Maybe I'll find it by your *next* birthday.

But what about *this* birthday?
I went back to my top secret plan
for an idea that would really blow
you away. That's when it hit me …

There were a few kinks to work out, and I was racing against time. So buckle up …

Because I got you a
'brand-new race car!

Except I forgot that you don't know how to drive yet. But you still need some way to get around.

How about a dinosaur?
Talk about a sweet ride.

Have you ever looked for a dinosaur? I couldn't find one anywhere.

Where did they all go?
My guess: outer space.

So then I bought you a rocket ship. You could explore space *and* find the dinosaurs.

But on my way home from the rocket ship store — *KABLAM!* Friendly martians crash-landed. I gave them your rocket ship to get home. You'd have done the same.

So here I am. I wanted to get you something amazing. Something unexpected. Something that you would really love.

Instead, I have nothing.

Nothing but ... **THIS STORY!**
It's the greatest present ever because
it's got all of the things you really love:

birthday socks

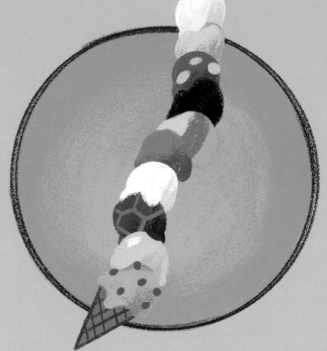

ice cream

rocking out

magic

apple juice

adventure

dinosaurs

friendly martians

Mike Erskine-Kellie & Susan McLennan • Cale Atkinson

Best of all, it's a story about you and me. So anytime you want, you can read it again and remember what great friends we are!

Now on to next year's gift ...

Dedicated to my mum and dad for building a house
of books, to my brother John for sharing his terrific insights,
to Katie Scott for being a totally awesome editor and
to Susan for lighting my life with love — M.E-K.

To my parents, Adrienne, Ian and Mr. A., for always being there; to
Sheila Barry for being the guiding star that she was; to Sharon Barwick
and Diana Birrell, who are two of the finest people I know;
and to my beloved Mike, who has given me a world filled
with more love than I ever thought possible — S.M.

To my parents for always spoiling me with
the perfect presents growing up — C.A.

Text © 2020 Mike Erskine-Kellie and Susan McLennan
Illustrations © 2020 Cale Atkinson

Kids Can Press gratefully acknowledges the financial support
of the Government of Ontario, through Ontario Creates; the
Ontario Arts Council; the Canada Council for the Arts; and the
Government of Canada for our publishing activity.

Published in Canada and the U.S. by Kids Can Press Ltd.
25 Dockside Drive, Toronto, ON M5A 0B5

Kids Can Press is a Corus Entertainment Inc. company

www.kidscanpress.com

The artwork in this book was rendered in cake icing, gorilla
vanilla ice cream and Photoshop.
The text is set in Futura Book.

Edited by Katie Scott
Designed by Julia Naimska

Printed and bound in Shenzhen, China, in 10/2019
by C&C Offset

CM 20 0 9 8 7 6 5 4 3 2 1

Library and Archives Canada Cataloguing in Publication

Title: I got you a present! / written by Mike Erskine-Kellie and
Susan McLennan ; illustrated by Cale Atkinson.
Names: Erskine-Kellie, Mike, author. | McLennan, Susan Eleni,
author. | Atkinson, Cale, illustrator.
Identifiers: Canadiana 2019008507X | ISBN 9781525300097
(hardcover)
Classification: LCC PS8609.R75 I36 2020 | DDC jC813/.6 —
dc23